Look for more books
in the GOOSEBUMPS PRESENTS series:

Goosebumps®

PRESENTS

GHOST BEACH

Adapted by Carol Ellis
From the teleplay by Jeffrey Cohen
Based on the novel by R.L. Stine

SCHOLASTIC INC.
New York Toronto London Auckland Sydney

A PARACHUTE PRESS BOOK

Adapted by Carol Ellis, from the screenplay by Jeffrey Cohen.
Based on the novel by R.L. Stine.

ISBN 0-590-29994-8

12 11 10 9 8 7 6 5 4 3 2 1   7 8 9/9 0 1 2/0

Printed in the U.S.A.   40

First Scholastic Printing, June 1997

1

"Terri!" I called. "Where are you? Terri!"

My sister didn't answer.

I glanced around the graveyard. Tall weeds grew everywhere. The tombstones were half-buried in moss. They stuck out of the dirt at weird angles. Fog drifted across the ground.

Even though it was a warm summer morning, I shivered. Cemeteries give me the creeps. Lots of things give me the creeps. Terri says I'm a wimp. Maybe I am. But I really wanted to get out of this place.

My name is Jerry Sadler. I'm twelve and Terri is eleven. Our parents didn't have time for a vacation this summer — so they stayed in our apartment in the city. They sent us to visit Dad's cousins, Brad and Agatha. Brad and Agatha are really old, but they're lots of fun. They live in a cool little house near the beach. I love the beach!

Terri and I were supposed to be on the beach right now. But on the way there, she found this creepy cemetery.

And now I'd lost her somewhere in the middle of it.

"Terri!" I called again.

She still didn't answer.

Where was my sister? I glanced around again.

No sign of her.

A dog barked in the distance. Then the bark turned into a howl. A long, wailing, spooky cry.

"Terri!" I shouted. "Terri!"

"Over here!" Terri's voice came from the other side of the cemetery.

Finally, I thought. Now we can get out of here.

I hurried through the weeds and moss. I

spotted Terri. She was on her knees next to one of the old tombstones. She held a piece of thin paper over the stone with one hand. With the other, she rubbed a wax crayon sideways across the paper.

"Oh, man!" I said. "You and your dumb hobbies. What did you do, bring paper and crayons in your backpack?"

Terri just kept rubbing the crayon over the paper.

"Grave rubbings. Who makes grave rubbings?" I kidded her.

"I do," she said without looking up. "*I'm* interested in lots of things — especially old, historic stuff. *You* never want to do anything."

"I do, too," I argued.

"Oh, yeah? Like what?"

"Like go to the beach," I reminded her. "We finally get to visit Brad and Agatha and all you want to do is rub gravestones."

"It's cool," Terri told me. She held up the paper. On it was the image of a skull that had been carved into the tombstone. A skull with wings sticking out of its head. "See, Jerry? It's an old Puritan symbol. A death's-head. Creepy, huh?"

Terri grinned. She knew I got scared by stuff like skulls. "Let's go to the beach," I said again.

Terri pointed to the tombstone. "Check out the name."

I peered at the letters carved in the mossy stone. "Harrison Sadler," I read. "Sadler!"

Terri grinned. "I know. And look." She pointed to the date on the tombstone. "He died in 1642. One of the first guys to come to America, and he's got *our* last name."

"Whoa!"

"And look at the words carved on the tombstone," she said. She took a big breath and read in a deep, dramatic voice. "'Though His Bones Are But Dust, His Spirit Lives On Forever.'"

Off in the distance, the dog howled again. "Come on, Terri," I said quickly. "Don't you want to go to the beach?"

She kept staring at the tombstone. "I love

4

it that everything around here is so old," she murmured. Then she glanced up.

Her eyes grew wide. Her face turned white. "Jerry!" she cried, pointing over my shoulder with a shaky finger.

I spun around.

Then I froze.

A figure burst out of a grave, right in front of me!

It was a hideous figure, covered with green, slimy moss. As it rose up, clumps of dirt fell from its head. Worms slithered through its hair. Its huge eyes glared at me.

My brain yelled at me to run, but my legs wouldn't move.

All I could do was scream in terror.

The monster from the grave stretched out its long bony fingers — and grabbed me!

2

The monster's fingers grabbed my shirt. Then it opened its dusty lips and let out an eerie wail.

"Help!" I screamed at Terri. But she stood frozen in fear.

I tried to twist away, but the monster from the grave held me tight. Its angry, wailing shriek rose higher and higher. "Help!" I screamed again.

But then, the wailing changed. The monster let go of my shirt — and began to howl with laughter. Stunned, I stumbled backward into Terri. We both fell against Harrison Sadler's tombstone.

Suddenly, a boy about my age leaped out

from behind another stone. He bounded over to the laughing monster and helped it up from the ground.

The monster brushed the dirt out of its hair and pulled clumps of moss from its face.

I stared. It wasn't a monster. It was a girl about Terri's age. She and the boy whooped with laughter.

"That was the best joke ever!" the boy cried.

I couldn't believe it! The whole thing was a lousy joke? I glared at the boy. "You're crazy if you think that was funny!" I told him angrily.

"We've been watching you guys," he said, as he tried to stop laughing.

"We saw you heading for the graveyard," the girl added. "So we thought we'd give you a little scare."

"*Little* scare?" I snapped.

The girl bit her lip and glanced at the boy. "I told you we shouldn't have done it, Sam."

"Let's get out of here, Terri." I grabbed my sister's arm, and we started moving away.

"Hey. We're sorry," Sam said.

"We are. We're really sorry," the girl repeated.

"It was just a joke," Sam explained.

Terri frowned. "A pretty dumb joke."

"I guess it was," Sam admitted. He smiled. "My name's Sam Sadler. This is my sister Louisa."

"Sadler?" Terri cried. "That's *our* last name!"

"Really?" Louisa looked surprised.

"Yeah. I'm Terri Sadler and this is my brother, Jerry," Terri told them.

Sam smiled again. I wasn't that mad anymore, so I smiled back. "We're staying with Brad and Agatha," I explained. "They're our fourth cousins, twice remodeled."

"*Removed*, Jerry," Terri said. She loves to correct me when I get things wrong. "Twice *removed*."

"Yeah," I agreed. "Whatever that means."

Terri rolled her eyes. "It means that they're distant relatives. They're Sadlers, too."

8

"Right. We know them," Sam told us. "Actually, there are lots of Sadlers in this town."

"No kidding." Terri pointed to Harrison Sadler's tombstone. "Even dead ones."

Sam and Louisa glanced at each other, then at us. "Harrison Sadler is dead," Louisa whispered in a frightened voice. "But he still walks the night."

Huh? Terri and I stared at each other.

"They're just trying to scare us again," I told her. I turned back to Sam and Louisa. "Nice try."

Sam and Louisa exchanged another glance. They didn't look as if they were joking this time. I couldn't believe it. Did they actually think the ghost of Harrison Sadler walked the night?

"Oh, come on!" I said.

"You don't really believe in ghosts, do you?" Terri asked.

Sam nodded. "If you go near the cave down at the beach, you will, too."

Sam and Louisa both looked so serious, I

started to feel a little spooked. "What cave?" I asked.

"Don't talk about it anymore, Sam," Louisa said quickly. She turned to us. "We'll see you around."

After Sam and Louisa walked off, Terri and I stared at each other. "Weird!" we both muttered at the same time.

In the distance, the dog began to howl again.

I glanced around. Sam and Louisa had disappeared into the thick mist. Even though the sun was out, the graveyard stayed dark.

Dark and scary.

As the howling filled the air, a chill ran down my spine.

3

"Agatha, give Jerry a little more pot pie," Brad said to his wife. We were all sitting around the kitchen table at lunch that day.

"I sure will, Brad." Agatha began to spoon up some beef pot pie. She's a tiny old woman, with white hair and wrinkled skin. She loves cooking. "It all tastes so much better cooked on the old wood stove," she added.

Brad nodded and stuffed a huge forkful of pie into his mouth. For such a skinny, old man, he can really shovel in the food! "The town has power lines," he explained. "But we never hooked up to them."

Brad and Agatha aren't just old, I thought. They're old-fashioned. Sort of like their cottage. Instead of electricity, it has a wood stove and kerosene lamps. It's built of stone, with a kitchen, a living room, and one bedroom. Terri and I sleep in a tiny loft under the sloping roof.

Agatha plopped some more pot pie onto my plate. I glanced down at the huge chunks of meat swimming in gravy. I was hungry, but this was way too much!

"Um . . . I don't think I can eat all this," I said.

"Really?" Brad looked surprised.

So did Agatha. "Your parents didn't say you were such little eaters."

Little? I'd bust a gut if I ate this much food! "I guess I'm not used to such a big lunch. But it's good," I added quickly.

"It's really good," Terri agreed.

Agatha beamed. "It's so nice having young people around to enjoy our way of life," she declared. "So nice your folks sent you up here to be with your old cousins."

I nodded. "It sure is better than spending the summer in a sweaty apartment," I said.

"Dad told us all kinds of stories about being here when he was a kid," Terri added. "We always wanted to meet you guys."

Brad gulped down another giant mouthful of pot pie. "Your dad always cared about keeping this family together," he explained. "Always made the effort."

"We met some other Sadlers today," I told him. "Kids."

"Sam and Louisa," Terri added.

"Mmm-hmmm. Nice kids," Brad murmured. He forked up another giant mouthful.

"Are they our relatives, too?" Terri asked.

Brad shrugged. "Could be."

"Very, very distant — *if* they are," Agatha said.

"They kept talking about some ghost," I told them. "A ghost in a cave at the beach."

"Never heard of it," Brad snapped. He quickly shoved his chair back and stood up. "Well, I've got some chores to do."

Agatha jumped to her feet. "I'll help."

They hurried from the kitchen. Terri and I frowned at each other, confused.

Brad and Agatha usually talked a lot. And they asked us questions all the time. They wanted to know about school and sports and friends and stuff.

So why didn't they want to hear about Sam and Louisa? Or about something as interesting as ghosts!

Why had our cousins suddenly clammed up?

At the beach that afternoon, Terri waded into a small tidepool. "You can actually eat some kinds of seaweed," she announced. She reached down into the murky water and pulled out a handful of slimy seaweed. "It's full of vitamins."

"Full of bugs is more like it," I told her with a frown. I was getting bored. The water was too cold for swimming, and I was tired of looking for shells.

"Let's go see if we can find that cave with the ghost," I suggested.

Terri shoved the seaweed up to my face. I gasped and jumped backwards.

Terri laughed. She loves to scare me. "I want to keep studying the seaweed," she declared.

"Well, I'm going to go look for that cave by myself then," I announced.

A high, rocky cliff ran along the edge of the beach. Thick, twisted trees grew like scraggly hair on top of the cliff. As I walked, I gazed at the wall of rock. I couldn't see a cave anywhere.

I tripped over something in the sand. "Whoa!"

When I caught my balance, I glanced down — and screamed.

"What is it?" Terri called out. "What's wrong?"

I was too freaked out to answer.

Terri ran to my side and looked down. She gasped.

A skeleton lay in the sand.

A skeleton with every bone in place.

Leg bones. Ribs. Arms.

And a shiny skull with empty eye sockets.

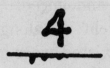

4

"Look at that!" My heart pounded and my voice was shaky. "A perfect skeleton."

"Weird," Terri murmured.

Weird? Spooky was more like it.

"Is it human?" Terri asked.

I forced myself to take a closer look. Whew! The skeleton was definitely not human. "Not unless humans have four legs, genius," I told her, pointing.

"Maybe a deer?" she suggested.

"Too small for a deer," a voice called out.

Terri and I jumped. We quickly glanced up.

A flat rock jutted out from the cliff just above our heads. Two figures sat on it, gazing down at us.

Sam and Louisa Sadler.

I frowned at them. "Do you guys always creep up on everyone?"

"Sorry," Sam said.

Terri kept staring at the bones. "If it's not a deer, what is it?"

"Just a dog," Sam told her.

"A dog?" Terri gasped. "Well, what happened to it?"

"It died, Terri," I said.

Sam shook his head. "No. It got eaten."

Louisa jabbed him with her elbow. "Sam!"

"Eaten? No way," I told him. "The bones are picked clean. I mean, what kind of animal would do something like this?"

Louisa glanced at Sam, then at me. "I guess if you're going to be around here, you should know — it wasn't an animal that picked those bones clean," she announced. "It was the ghost. The ghost of Harrison Sadler."

"Oh, come on!" I protested.

"It killed that dog and ate it," Louisa went on, "because dogs can tell if someone is a ghost."

"Dogs always bark to warn people about ghosts," Sam added.

"Give me a break!" I said.

Sam turned to Louisa. "Let's go."

"Wait a second," Terri told them. "Have you ever seen the ghost?"

"We —" Louisa started to say. But Sam grabbed her arm. "They don't believe us, Louisa," he told her. "Don't waste your time."

"They need to know, Sam," Louisa insisted. She pointed to the rocks above her. I gazed up and spotted a hole tucked behind two huge boulders.

"See that opening in the rocks?" Louisa asked. "The ghost lives in that cave. They say he's been there for hundreds of years."

"Have you ever seen him?" Terri asked again. She sounded interested, as usual.

"No one has," Louisa whispered.

"If you've never seen him, how do you know he's up there?" I demanded.

"We've seen other skeletons," Louisa told me.

"And the flickering light in the mouth of the cave," Sam added.

They sounded serious. Really serious. But I still didn't believe it. "It's probably just some guy with a flashlight," I muttered.

But gazing up at the rocks, I suddenly spotted something in the entrance of the cave.

An eerie, glowing light.

I blinked.

The light was still there.

Then the light began to flicker. "Huh?" I murmured. The light looked exactly the way Sam had described it.

"What's wrong with you, Jerry?" Terri asked.

Sam's eyes were wide with fear. "You saw the light, didn't you? The light the ghost makes."

"I'm not sure," I muttered. But my hands felt clammy and my heart pounded. I had seen *something*, all right. But what?

Terri frowned at Sam and Louisa. "This is another one of your dumb jokes, isn't it?"

Sam glared at her. "Think what you want," he snapped. "Come on, Louisa. I told you they didn't believe us!"

I watched the two of them stomp off into the woods. Then I glanced up at the cave entrance again.

The flickering light had disappeared.

What was it? I wondered. A flashlight? A trick of the sunlight?

Or a ghost?

5

"I made some nice beef stew," Agatha said that night at dinner. Smiling, she spooned some onto my plate.

I looked down. One piece of meat, one bite of potato, a slice of carrot, and three peas. "I can eat more than that, Agatha," I told her.

Agatha clicked her tongue. "I just don't know how much to serve you kids," she said. "First you're not hungry, now you are."

She spooned another helping onto my plate. This time it was a giant helping. I knew I could never eat it all, but I decided not to say anything.

Agatha turned to Terri. "How about you?"

"About half of what you gave Jerry will be fine," Terri told her.

Agatha chuckled and plopped a big spoonful of stew onto Terri's plate.

Terri held up her hand. "That's plenty."

"So what did you two do this afternoon?" Brad asked.

"We saw those kids again. You know — Sam and Louisa Sadler?" I took a sip of milk. "They told us more about that ghost in the cave. They said it kills things and eats dogs. And it makes this light go off and on."

"Yeah." Terri snickered. "Jerry thinks he saw a ghost."

"I did not. I didn't see a ghost," I protested. At least, I didn't think I did. "I did see a light," I admitted.

Agatha glanced at Brad. She looked worried.

Brad shook his head at her, then looked at me. "Ever hear of aurora borealis, Jerry?" he asked.

I nodded. "Yeah."

Brad polished off his first helping of stew

and spooned up a second. "Happens certain times of the year. Something electric gets in the air, and the whole sky lights up in streamers. Maybe that's what you saw."

"It was the middle of the day," I argued.

Brad shook a bony finger at me. "You just stay clear of beach caves, you hear me?" he ordered. "I don't want you kids coming home with any broken bones!"

Whoa! I thought as I glanced at Terri. Brad didn't sound mad, exactly. But he sure sounded nervous.

What was going on?

Late that night, I slipped out of bed and quietly pulled on my jeans. Moonlight streamed through the curtains. It was almost as bright as day in the tiny sleeping loft.

I yanked a hooded sweatshirt over my head. In the distance, a dog barked. Terri shuffled and muttered in her sleep.

The barking turned to a loud howl.

Terri sat up.

I put my hand on her shoulder. She gasped, frightened.

"Shhh. It's me," I whispered.

"Are you nuts?" she asked loudly.

"Ssshhh!" I hissed. "You'll wake up Brad and Agatha. Listen, do you feel like checking out that cave?"

"It's the middle of the night," she complained.

"I know, but I can't sleep. I keep thinking about that light I saw," I told her. "Come on, Terri, where's your sense of adventure?"

"I don't know." She yawned. "Where's your sense of night and day?"

The dog barked again. Then the barks turned into yelps. Yelps of pain.

I winced at the sound. "Do you hear that?" I asked.

Terri nodded and bit her lip. "Yeah."

"Do you think the ghost got it?"

She quickly shook her head. "I don't believe in ghosts."

"Well, neither do I," I told her. "But *some-*

thing's going on. You saw Brad and Agatha. They know something about that cave — only they don't want to tell us."

Terri nodded. "They probably don't want us to get scared."

"Well, don't you want to find out what the big secret is?" I demanded.

Terri looked unsure. "Yeah. But I don't know if we should."

"Come on," I pleaded. "I go with you when you do your creepy grave rubbings and your gross seaweed junk. What about doing something I want to do for a change?"

"I'm kind of scared," she admitted.

"Me, too," I said. Then I grinned. "That's why it's fun."

Terri finally agreed. She quickly got dressed. Then we tiptoed down past Agatha and Brad's bedroom, and slipped quietly out of the cottage.

We followed a winding path through the woods. Soon we were running along the sandy beach. When we reached the base of the cliff, we began to climb. Slowly we worked our way up the steep, wet rocks toward the mouth of the cave.

We were almost there. Suddenly Terri slipped.

She grabbed onto a rock, but her feet dangled in the air.

"Jerry, help!" she cried. Her hands were starting to slip.

Just in time, I reached out and grabbed her arm. She kicked against the rock and finally found a toehold.

"Be careful," I whispered. I dragged her up beside me.

We sat down to rest. Terri took a shaky breath. "Jerry, what if there really is a ghost?" she whispered.

I glanced around. The night was chilly. Wispy gray clouds floated across the full moon. A perfect night for a ghost, I thought. A shiver ran down my spine. You don't believe in ghosts, I reminded myself. Don't wimp out now!

"There are no ghosts," I told Terri. "It's something else. It's got to be."

"Look!" Terri cried, pointing.

As I glanced up, I felt that shiver run down my spine again.

A light floated in the dark mouth of the cave.

An eerie, flickering light.

It was the same light I'd seen before. The light Sam said was a ghost!

6

My mouth felt dry. I swallowed hard. "That's no aurora boring alice," I whispered.

"Aurora borealis," Terri corrected me.

"Yeah." I swallowed again. "Well, that's not it. Come on," I told her.

I stood up. I wedged the toe of my sneaker between two rocks. Then I grabbed hold of a tree root sticking out above me, and hauled myself up a few more feet. I reached down and grabbed Terri's hand. I pulled her up next to me.

We both glanced up. The flickering light had grown brighter. We kept scrambling toward it. The closer we got, the brighter it grew.

My name is Jerry Sadler. My sister, Terri, and I were visiting our dad's cousins, Brad and Agatha, for the summer. They live in a cottage near the shore.

The Remains of

HARRISON SADLER

Though his bones are but dust, his spirit lives on forever. 1642

One day, on our way to the beach, we found a creepy graveyard. Terri pointed to a headstone that said *Harrison Sadler*. "Maybe he was one of our ancestors," she said.

Just then something weird burst out of a grave behind us! Aaaaah!

It was just a girl playing a joke on us. She told us her name was Louisa Sadler. She said there were *lots* of Sadlers in this town!

Louisa introduced us to her brother, Sam. They told us Harrison Sadler had been dead for three hundred years. But his ghost haunted the town.

Sam and Louisa had never seen the ghost, but they said he lived in a cave near the beach. It sounded like a stupid story to me. I don't believe in ghosts.

The next night I woke up my sister after everyone else was asleep. I wanted to go to the cave—to *prove* that there was no ghost living up there.

Terri and I snuck out of the house. We walked to the beach in the dark. Then we climbed up the high cliff to the cave.

We couldn't believe what we found. The ghost! The ghost of Harrison Sadler.
He was real!

Harrison spoke to us. He said he wasn't a ghost. He said Sam and Louisa were! We didn't know who was telling the truth.

Harrison told us there was a terrible surprise for us in the graveyard. We ran down there. And you won't believe what we found....

In memory of

JERRY SADLER

Headstones with *our* names on them! Oh, no! Now someone wanted to turn *us* into ghosts. But who was it? Harrison Sadler? Or Sam and Louisa?

Finally, we dragged ourselves onto a ledge. We were right at the mouth of the cave.

The light was close now. Close enough to touch.

I took a deep breath and stuck my hand out toward it.

The light grew even brighter. Suddenly it flickered away from my hand and began to go into the cave.

"Did you see that?" I gasped.

"Yes." Terri's voice shook.

"Oh, man, this is amazing!" I muttered. My mouth had gone dry again. But even though I was scared, I was excited, too. I *had* to find out what was going on!

I took a deep breath. Then I stepped into the cave. Terri followed me.

I gazed around. Ahead of me stretched a long, dark tunnel. Water dripped from its ceiling and oozed down its sides. The rocky floor was wet. It was dark and damp and creepy. Definitely not my kind of place.

But I could see the flickering light in the distance. I had to find out what it was!

I made myself take a step forward on the slippery rocks.

Then another and another. I followed the flickering light deeper and deeper into the cave.

The tunnel turned and twisted. The air became colder. The dripping water felt icy. Terri coughed. "I'm freezing," she moaned.

Up ahead, the light darted around a curve in the tunnel and disappeared. After a few seconds, it reappeared. It floated in the distance, as if it were waiting. "It's taking us somewhere!" I cried.

The light darted around the curve again. I started to run after it, when suddenly I heard a noise. I stopped. "Listen! You hear that?"

Terri coughed again. "I'm too busy trying to breathe."

I stood still, listening. There it was again. A soft, chittering sound. Squeaky. Sort of like a bunch of mice, I thought.

The squeaking grew louder. Then I heard a rustling noise. It came from above us.

I glanced up.

And screamed.

Bats! There were bats hanging from the ceiling! There were thousands of them. I could see their shiny black wings and glowing red eyes.

I could also see their sharp, gleaming fangs.

Run! I told myself. Get out of here before those fangs rip you apart! But before I could move, the bats began to drop straight down onto our heads!

I screamed again. Terri shrieked. Then we both fell to the ground and covered our heads with our hands.

The bats swooped around us, flapping and squeaking so loud I could hardly hear myself scream. Their claws plucked at my sweatshirt. Their wings flapped against my head.

We'll never get away from them! I thought. We'll never get out of his tunnel!

I screamed in terror, louder than ever.

And suddenly, the squeaking and the flapping went away. The tunnel became quiet again. All I could hear was dripping water and Terri gasping for breath.

I peeked out from between my fingers. A soft yellow light surrounded us.

"Are they gone?" Terri whimpered.

I glanced up. No bats. "I think so." I got to my knees and looked around. "Whoa! Terri!" I cried. "Look at this!"

Just ahead, the tunnel opened into a large stone room. Hundreds of candles stood in a circle on the floor. They surrounded an old, driftwood table.

Hunched over the table sat a tall, bony man. Stringy white hair hung from his head. His eyes were sunk deep in his skull-like face.

A skeleton! I thought.

A ghost!

My heart pounded in my ears. My knees turned to jelly.

As Terri and I stood frozen in terror, the man raised a bony finger and crooked it at us. His bloodless lips opened. "Come here," he croaked in a dry, dusty voice.

We couldn't move.

I stared in horror as the man slowly rose from the table. His sunken eyes glared at me.

Then he took a step forward. And another.

He's coming after us! I thought. If he catches us, he'll kill us!

With a gasp, I spun around and gave Terri a shove. We both raced back into the tunnel. I could hear footsteps behind us. The old man was chasing us!

We can outrun him, I thought. We have to! I grabbed Terri's hand. Together we tore through the damp, dripping tunnel. Faster and faster.

Suddenly I tripped. I crashed to my knees on the slippery rocks.

Terri kept running. Good. Maybe she could get help.

I tried to scramble up, but I slipped again. I fell onto my stomach. The man's footsteps grew louder. Closer.

I flipped over onto my back.

The man loomed over me, glaring.

His bony, twisted hands reached out for me.

"Nooo!" I screamed.

7

I backed away from the old man as fast as I could. But as I started to scramble up, I bumped into Terri. She had come back to help me.

My sister froze in terror as the man's lips twisted into an evil grin.

"I'm not going to eat you," he told her. Then he lurched toward us again.

"Terri! Run!" I yelled, leaping to my feet.

Terri jumped. Then she raced after me as I fled into the tunnel.

There was no more light to guide us. The tunnel was black.

"It's so dark! I can't see!" Terri yelled, breathing heavily.

"He'll kill us!" I shouted at her over my shoulder. "Go! Go! GO!"

We kept racing through the twisting tunnel, scraping our fingers on the rocky walls. I could hear the man's footsteps behind us. Clattering on the wet floor. Chasing us. Gaining on us!

Then a dim light appeared ahead. It grew brighter as we ran toward it. And then I could see a sliver of moonlight.

It's the entrance to the cave! I thought in relief. The way out! "There!" I shouted.

Terri suddenly screamed. I turned around just in time to see the old man grab her. And before I could do anything, he stretched out a long, bony arm and grabbed me, too.

"Let go!" I hollered.

The man's sunken eyes glared at me. "Quiet!" he roared. I bit my lip, too scared to scream any more. "You're coming with me!" he ordered.

Gripping our arms tightly, he dragged us back through the tunnel. He pulled us into the candlelit chamber. Then he let go and stood at the entrance, blocking our way out.

I glanced at the driftwood table. On it sat an old tin bowl, a frying pan, and a couple of bent spoons.

There was also an axe.

A very big, very sharp axe.

"You're both in serious trouble," the man declared in his dry, raspy voice.

Terri stared at the axe, then at him. "What are you going to do to us?" she whispered.

"It's dangerous to get involved with ghosts," he warned.

"We didn't mean any harm," I told him.

"No?" He frowned. "You're trying to trap me, aren't you?"

Terri shook her head. "No!"

"Admit it!" he demanded.

"We were just looking around!" I insisted. "Honest. Why would we want to trap you?"

The man moved slowly across the chamber toward us. Then he leaned down until his skull-like face was inches from ours. His sunken eyes glared at us.

"Do you think I'm a ghost?" he whispered fiercely.

We were too afraid to answer. We were almost too afraid to breathe.

"My name is Harrison Sadler," he went on. "I traveled here from England a number of years ago."

Terri nodded. "Three hundred and fifty years ago," she said in a shaky voice. "I saw your gravestone."

Harrison shook his head. "Not *my* gravestone. Another Harrison Sadler's. A very *old* Harrison Sadler's." His lips twisted in a creepy grin. "I'm going to tell you a story. I want you to listen very carefully."

Terri and I glanced at each other. We were trapped. We had to listen, whether we wanted to or not.

"In the year sixteen hundred and forty-one a group of Pilgrims sailed from England to begin a new life here," Harrison said. "But when they finally arrived, it was winter. A freezing, terrible winter. They had no real shelter. Not enough food. They grew so cold, so hungry, their blood practically froze in their veins. And one by one — they died!"

Harrison shook his head, a sad expression on his face. "Their deaths were so awful, so painful, that some refused to go to their final resting place," he continued softly. "And so they stayed."

"Like you?" Terri asked.

"I told you!" Harrison snapped angrily. "I'm no ghost!"

"Then why did you drag us here?" I asked.

"To warn you!" he told us. "I study ghosts. I'm not a ghost — but your two young friends are!"

Terri's eyes grew wide. "Sam and Louisa?"

"Dead for three hundred years," Harrison declared. "I've studied them. I've seen their evil."

No way, I thought. "You're the ghost!" I told him, glancing around. "Shut up in this dark old cave."

"The cave is my hideaway!" he cried. "The only safe place for me. The ghosts know I'm watching, but they can't come in here. And I dare not leave."

"But Sam and Louisa are just kids — kids like us," I argued.

"They're not evil," Terri agreed.

Harrison didn't speak. He just stared at us.

"What are you going to do?" I finally asked him.

"Let you go," he announced with a sigh.

"Why?" Terri asked.

"Because you won't listen to me!" he cried.

Terri glanced at the axe again. "He's going to kill us, Jerry," she whispered in terror.

Harrison shook his head. "Go back to the graveyard," he told us. "To the northeastern corner. You'll find your answer there."

We didn't move. Was he actually going to let us go?

"To the graveyard!" Harrison shouted. He pointed a bony finger toward the tunnel. "Now!"

We ran into the tunnel, and didn't stop running until we were out of the cave.

"Oh, man!" Terri gasped when we got outside.

"This is crazy!" I cried. "Wait. Slow down!"

Panting, we stopped and looked back at the cave.

"I don't know what to believe!" Terri murmured.

I shook my head in confusion. "Me neither!"

"Do you think he's a ghost?" she asked.

I shrugged. "He says Sam and Louisa are the ghosts."

"But maybe he's lying," Terri argued.

Maybe, I thought. But maybe not. "We've got to go to the graveyard," I told her.

Terri shook her head. "I don't want to."

"We've got to check it out," I insisted. "The northeastern corner. That's what he said, right?"

Terri took a shaky breath. "Okay," she agreed. "The northeastern corner."

I nodded, and we began climbing down the rocks.

A dog barked in the distance.

I shuddered. The cemetery was the last place I wanted to go.

But I had to find out the truth.

8

The tilting tombstones cast spooky shadows in the moonlight.

Terri pointed. "The ocean is behind us, so northeast is this way."

We started walking. A few seconds later, I grabbed her arm. "What was that?" I asked quietly.

"What?"

"I thought I heard something," I whispered. I held my breath and listened. All I heard was the wind rustling through the weeds, and the distant whoosh of waves on the beach.

I let my breath out. "Are we in the north-eastern corner?" I asked.

She nodded. "We should be."

We moved through the cemetery a few more feet. Then I grabbed her arm again. "Terri. Look!"

I pointed to two chipped, mossy gravestones. Each one had a name carved on it. "Louisa Sadler and Samuel Sadler," I read.

"Wow!" Terri gasped. "This must be it, right?" she asked nervously. "What he wanted us to see? Right?"

"Yeah," I agreed. "Harrison Sadler was right. Sam and Louisa died three hundred years ago. They *are* ghosts! This is getting weirder all the time!"

"Hey!" a voice called out.

I jumped and whirled around. Sam and Louisa stood there, staring at us.

Terri and I took a step backwards.

"I'm glad you guys are okay," Sam told us.

"We've been looking for you," Louisa added.

Terri and I glanced at each other. Were they telling the truth? "What are you doing here?" I asked.

"We heard you in the woods," Louisa explained. "Are you all right?"

"We saw him!" Terri announced.

"Who?" Sam asked.

"The ghost," she told him.

Sam's eyes grew wide with fear. "Oh, no!"

I nodded. "We saw him in the cave. He really lives in there."

Louisa frowned. "We've been here all our lives and we never saw him."

"Well, we did!" Terri insisted.

"Did he see you?" Louisa asked.

Terri nodded. "Yeah."

Sam shook his head. "That's not good."

"How did you get away?" Louisa asked me.

"He let us go." I stared at them. "He said he's *not* a ghost."

Sam and Louisa rolled their eyes. I could tell they didn't believe us.

"He told us to come here. To look for something," Terri told them.

"Look for what?" Louisa demanded.

Terri raised her hand and pointed. "Your gravestones."

Sam and Louisa looked at the stones. Then Sam whistled. "The ghost is clever," he said. "He wants you to think *we're* the ghosts."

"And you believe him!" Louisa cried. "You do. I can tell by your faces!"

Terri pointed to the stones again. "If you're not ghosts, then why are your names carved into these tombstones?" she demanded.

"Those stones aren't ours. The graves belong to two of our relatives from a long time ago," Louisa explained. "We just got named after them, that's all."

Sam turned away and began walking deeper into the graveyard. "Now we're going to show *you* something," he called over his shoulder. "This is why we were looking for you. Come here. Let me show you what the ghost is planning for you."

"What?" Terri asked. She didn't move. Neither did I. We were too afraid.

"Go on!" Louisa pushed us ahead of her. "You need to see it. You have to believe us!"

Louisa herded us toward Sam. He stood looking down at something.

"What is it?" Terri asked as we got closer.

Sam just kept staring down. "Look," he urged.

We slowly followed Sam's gaze.

Terri and I both gasped in horror.

There at our feet were two long, gaping holes in the ground. These holes were big enough to lie down in. Fresh dirt was piled at the sides. Spooky tombstones stood at the ends.

There were two names carved in the tombstones.

Our names.

Jerry Sadler and Terri Sadler.

9

"*Our* graves?" I asked in a shaky voice.

Sam nodded. "For you and your sister. This is what the ghost didn't want you to see. He used his magic to dig them."

"What does he want?" Terri whispered, sounding scared.

"What do you think?" Louisa asked. "To eat you and bury your bones right here." She stared at me. "He saw you, Jerry. He'll come out of the cave and find you."

"No, he won't," Terri cried.

"Yes, he will!" Sam insisted in a fierce voice. "He won't rest until he gets you!"

"Stop it!" I shouted, as Terri began to cry. "You're scaring her!"

"I don't mean to," Louisa said quickly. "But you have to understand. Your lives are in danger!"

"So . . ." Terri gulped. "So what do you think we should do?"

"Get rid of the ghost," Sam told her. "Stop his evil once and for all."

Terri frowned. "How are we supposed to do that?"

"Seal him up in his cave with rocks," Louisa said.

"Rocks? But he's a ghost!" I protested. "Can't he float through stuff?"

"The legend says the cave is a safe hideaway," Louisa explained.

"If something evil gets trapped inside, it can't get out," Sam added. "So that's what you have to do. Trap the ghost."

"Remember, Jerry?" Terri said to me. "That's what he thought you were trying to do. Trap him."

"I guess he *is* a ghost," I agreed.

Louisa nodded. "You have to attack him, before he attacks you."

"But if he's evil, why haven't you done it already?" I asked them.

Sam shook his head. "We live here. If we mess up, the ghost won't stop at killing us," he explained. "He'll haunt our house, our family. He'll get revenge *forever*."

"You saw your graves. You want to live, don't you?" Louisa stared at me. "Well, don't you?"

I glanced down at the two fresh graves and shuddered.

I definitely wanted to live!

And that meant only one thing — we had to get rid of the ghost of Harrison Sadler.

10

Thunder rumbled loudly as the four of us stared up toward the cave. Sam waved for Terri and me to keep climbing. "We'll keep watch," he told us.

"No." No way will Terri and I go up there alone, I thought. "You come up with us," I insisted.

Louisa shook her head. "We can't do it, Jerry."

"You don't have to go inside the cave," Terri said. "Just wait outside, okay?"

Sam and Louisa frowned, but they kept climbing with us. In a few minutes, we were at the entrance to the cave. Thunder rumbled again, louder this time. Lightning flashed in the sky above us.

We all grabbed hold of a broken tree branch. Then we shoved the end under the big boulder next to the cave. If we could pry the boulder loose, we could roll it in front of the cave entrance.

We pushed down on the end of the branch. Then we lifted it and pushed down again. And again. Finally, the rock began to budge.

"Just a little more," I shouted over the sound of the thunder.

"Okay, Jerry," Sam shouted back.

With one more push, the boulder came free. As we started to roll it in front of the cave, a blinding bolt of lightning zapped from the sky. There was a loud crash as it hit the rock cliff.

The blast knocked us all to the ground. We lay there gasping. Rocks and dirt and huge chunks of stone slammed down around us.

Finally, the dust settled. I slowly got to my knees and looked up.

And screamed with terror.

Harrison Sadler stood in the cave entrance. In one skeleton-like hand, he held a flaming torch. He stared down at us, his pale lips forming an eerie smile.

"Well, well, well! Here we all are," he croaked in his hoarse voice. His sunken eyes burned into Terri. "You've done well, bringing the ghosts to me," he told her.

"Ghosts?" Sam cried. "Us?"

"You're the ghost!" Louisa insisted.

"Get him, Jerry!" Sam yelled to me. "Push him in!"

I was too confused to move. I didn't know what to do!

Harrison glared at Sam and Louisa. "You've terrified people long enough," he told them.

"Liar!" Louisa screamed.

I looked at Harrison. Then at Sam and Louisa. Who was lying? Which ones were the ghosts? I didn't know!

"Look at him, Jerry!" Sam demanded,

pointing at Harrison. "Look at his eyes. All alone in the dark for hundreds of years."

I glanced at Harrison again. He kept staring at Sam and Louisa. "I've waited so long for you," he told them.

"He's lying, Terri!" Louisa pleaded. "You have to destroy him!"

"Me?" Terri cried.

Harrison held the torch high and stepped toward Sam and Louisa. "It's time for you to rest," he said.

Sam and Louisa began to back toward the edge of the cliff. Just a few more steps, and they would get away!

Suddenly, Harrison let out a long, high-pitched whistle.

In seconds, a huge black dog bounded up onto the ledge. Sam and Louisa froze as it glared at them fiercely. Then it flattened its ears, peeled back its lips, and gave out a vicious growl.

"Get away!" Sam yelled at the dog.

"Get!" Louisa shrieked.

The dog snarled at them. Then it began to bark.

Suddenly I remembered something.

"You said it yourself, Louisa!" I cried. "Dogs recognize ghosts! Dogs *bark* at ghosts!"

Now I knew the truth. Sam and Louisa had been trying to trick us all along.

They were the real ghosts!

11

Louisa and Sam began to wail. Loud, eerie cries that sent shivers down my back.

"We never had a chance to live!" Louisa cried.

Harrison turned to the dog. "Now!" he commanded. "Bring them to me!" As another thunderclap blasted through the night, he lifted his torch and moved back into the cave.

Growling and barking, the dog advanced on Sam and Louisa. They moved backward. The dog kept coming toward them, backing them closer and closer to the cave. With each step, they screamed those eerie ghost wails.

"The first winter! It wasn't fair!" Sam cried.

Louisa sobbed. "We never had a life at all!"

"We all died in the cold!" Sam wailed.

"Hungry! We were so hungry!" Louisa whimpered.

I watched them back into the cave. I couldn't believe my eyes. Sam and Louisa had totally changed. They didn't look like humans anymore.

Instead, they were skeletons. Bones with no flesh. Talking skulls with eyes.

"Stay with us, cousins!" Louisa begged, waving her bony hands at us.

"Join us!" Sam's jawbone clicked as he pleaded. "We dug such nice graves for you! Stay with us! Please!"

"The dead shall remain dead!" Harrison cried. He lifted his torch, and another lightning bolt zapped from the sky. It slammed into the rocks above the cave.

"Nooo!" Sam and Louisa screamed.

Their screams were drowned out as more rocks crashed down. A cloud of dust covered the cave entrance.

Terri and I huddled together, horrified.

We couldn't see the mouth of the cave anymore. It had been totally sealed with rocks.

There was no sign of Harrison, Sam, Louisa, or the dog.

Terri huddled closer to me. "Jerry," she whispered. "Next time you see me sleeping — don't wake me up!"

By the time we got back to the cottage, the storm had stopped. Rain thundered on the roof as Terri and I sat next to the wood-burning stove to get dry. Wrapped in blankets, we drank cocoa and told Brad and Agatha everything that had happened.

"Sam and Louisa were always popping up out of nowhere, freaking us out," I explained.

"Louisa seemed so nice." Terri sighed.

"Well, that's quite a story, kids," Brad said.

"We're sorry for sneaking out like that," I told him.

Agatha shook her head. "We didn't even know you were gone."

"Nope, nope," Brad agreed, tying his

bathrobe tighter. "Well, I'd say you've had quite a fright."

"Oh yes, quite a fright," Agatha repeated. "But it's over now and best forgotten."

Agatha stood up and smoothed down her long nightgown. Suddenly a dog barked loudly outside.

I ran to the window and looked out. Standing near the front door was a huge black dog with glaring eyes.

"Harrison Sadler's dog!" I exclaimed. "He must have gotten out of the cave!"

Terri raced to the door and pulled it open.

The dog immediately began to growl.

"Easy boy, easy," Terri murmured.

The dog growled again.

"You must be really frightened, huh?" Terri asked him.

The dog kept growling.

But not at Terri or me. At Brad and Agatha.

"That's only Brad and Agatha," I told the dog. "Why are you growling at them?"

The dog ignored me. Still growling, it began to move toward Brad and Agatha.

"Bad dog! Bad dog!" Brad yelled at him. "Giving away our little secret like that."

Secret? I gasped. So did Terri.

Brad and Agatha were ghosts, too! That's why the dog was growling.

Our cousins were ghosts!

Slowly, Terri and I began to back across the room.

Agatha stared at the dog for a moment. Then her tiny eyes began to twinkle.

"Maybe he's not such a bad dog, Brad," she said. "In fact, he might be a very *good* dog."

Brad began to smile. "Well, it's a little early for breakfast, but..." He glanced at us. "Terri, Jerry, why don't you kids set the table while Agatha gets busy in the kitchen? And don't tell me you're not hungry!"

Breakfast? Ghosts *eat* dogs, I remembered.

Terri and I glanced at each other. Then we stared at the dog.

Breakfast! I thought in horror.

Reader Beware

My Best Friend Is Invisible
Goosebumps #57
by R.L. Stine   *144 pp.*
Sammy's new friend is "outta sight." His name is Brent Green. . . .
And he's invisible!

Escape from Camp Run-for-Your-Life
Give Yourself Goosebumps #19
by R.L. Stine   *144 pp.*

It's your first day of sports camp and you're psyched! You can enter
the strange athletic competition called the Selection or go on the
creepy wilderness hike. But no matter what choice you make, you're
doomed to find out why all the kids call it Camp <u>Run-for-Your-Life!</u>

You Can't Scare Me!
Goosebumps Presents TV Book #14
64 pp.
Courtney's not afraid of anything. She's not even scared when
Eddie's friend dresses up as the Mud Monster. But how brave will
Courtney be when the <u>real</u> Mud Monster shows up!

AVAILABLE WHEREVER YOU GET

Goosebumps®

Only $3.99 each!